For Keaton — D. J. M.

To Victoria — A. B.

THE MONSTER
Princess

Written by
D. J. MACHALE

Illustrated by
ALEXANDRA
BOIGER

aladdin

An imprint of Simon & Schuster Children's Publishing Division

1230 Avenue of the Americas, New York, NY 10020

First Aladdin hardcover edition August 2010

Text copyright © 2010 by D. J. MacHale

Illustrations copyright © 2010 by Alexandra Boiger

For information about special discounts for bulk purchases, please contact Simon & Schuster Special Sales

at 1-866-506-1949 or business@simonandschuster.com.

The Simon & Schuster Speakers Bureau can bring authors to your live event. For more information

or to book an event contact the Simon & Schuster Speakers Bureau at 1-866-248-3049

or visit our website at www.simonspeakers.com.

Designed by Karin Paprocki

The text of this book was set in Truedell Regular.

Manufactured in China

0610 SCP

2 4 6 8 10 9 7 5 3

Library of Congress Cataloging-in-Publication Data

MacHale, D. J.

The monster princess / by D. J. MacHale ; illustrated by Alexandra Boiger. — 1st Aladdin ed.

p. cm.

Summary: Unhappy with her life in a dark cave, Lala longs to live like the princesses far,

far above, but after venturing into their world, she finds contentment at home.

ISBN 978-1-4169-4809-4 (alk. paper)

[1. Stories in rhyme. 2. Self-acceptance—Fiction. 3. Contentment—Fiction. 4. Monsters—Fiction. 5. Princesses—Fiction.]

I. Boiger, Alexandra, ill. II. Title.

PZ8.3.M1596Mon 2010

[E]—dc22

2008037933

THE MONSTER

Princess

aladdin   NEW YORK   LONDON   TORONTO   SYDNEY

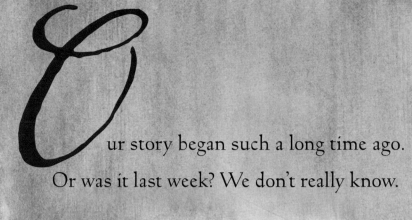

*O*ur story began such a long time ago.
Or was it last week? We don't really know.

A mountaintop castle was home to three girls.

Pretty young princesses.

Shiny, bright pearls.

These maidens were precious as twelve-carat gems.

However, this tale is not about them.

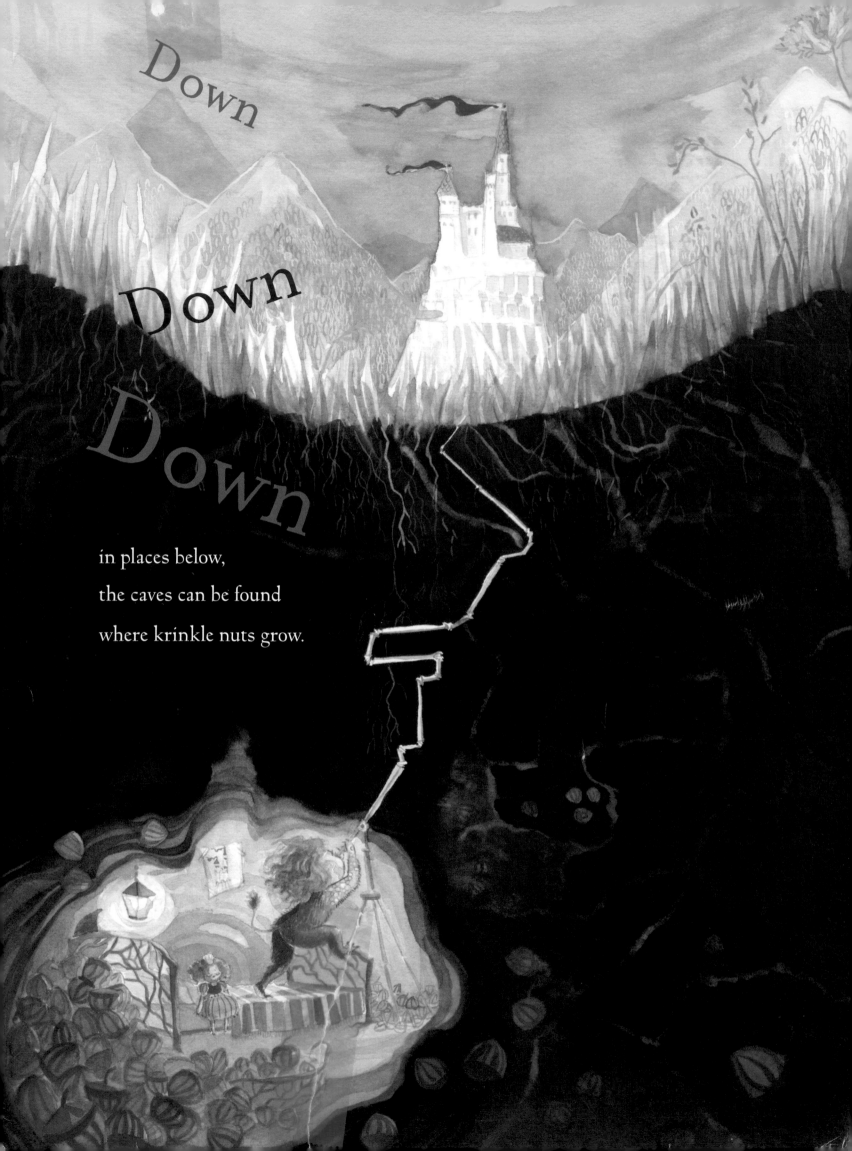

Down

Down

Down

in places below,
the caves can be found
where krinkle nuts grow.

This world full of monsters is quiet and gloomy.

It's dark.

It's spooky.

It's not very roomy.

The creatures who dwell there are called rugabees.

They dig up the krinkles and fight off the fleas.

The best krinkle-digger was Lala, by far.

So fast.

So brave.

A rugabee star.

But living in shadow just wasn't her style.
She wanted some light! (For more than a while.)
A princess is what Lala wanted to be,
for they sang and danced,
while she lived with fleas.

Her mom kissed her cheek and said, "Try not to care
about rings on your toes and the clothes that you wear."
She called her sweet daughter
        My Star Who Shines Bright.
But Lala felt more like a gnome trapped in night.
She wanted to dance! She wanted to play!
She needed to fly,
        and today was the day!

Up Up Up Up

from the dark of her home
she began an adventure
to face the unknown.

In the castle, a chance!
The girls weren't around.
She crept to their room
and tried on their gowns.

The dresses weren't hers.
She knew it was wrong.
But they made her feel special . . .
so she stayed way too long.

"A monster!"

"Our dresses!"

"You're stinky!"

"Get out!"

The girls all near fainted
and would have, no doubt,
but Lala cried, "Sorry!
I just want a chance
to live like a princess.
To dress up and dance."

The princesses stopped all their shouting and fuss.

"You want to be special? A princess? Like us?"

"Yes!" Lala begged. "I may look like a brute,

but with dresses and jewelry I could be quite cute."

The princesses huddled and hatched a great plan.

"All right!" they announced. "We'll do what we can!"

What followed was magic, a rare dream come true.

"Relax," the girls said. "We know just what to do."

So they scrubbed her and clipped her and brushed out the grime.

From monster
to princess
in next to no time.

"To the ball!" they declared.
Lala smiled with delight.
"There's a ball?" she squealed.
"In the castle? Tonight?"

When she entered the hall,
it was perfect and bright.

But the ending was not to be

happy that night.

Everyone stared with eyes open wide
at the brown little monster who shuffled inside.
She wanted to dance, but her claws ripped the gown.

She
stumbled,

and
bumbled,

and
finally
fell
down.

The people all gaped at the pitiful scene.

One laughed. Then another.

And the sisters turned mean.

"You're not special at all!" one barked with a sneer.

"You're a monster forever. Now get out of here!"

It was all a cruel trick, from the end to the start.

Such a horrible joke that broke Lala's heart.

Down

Down

Down

she fled back to her room.

She wanted it dark.

She welcomed the gloom.

"I belong in this cave, forever a troll.

Doomed to a life in this shadowy hole."

All that was left of her hopes was the gown,

the torn, tattered dress that brought her dream down.

The gown wasn't hers.

Never was, she now knew.

Which meant she had something important to do.

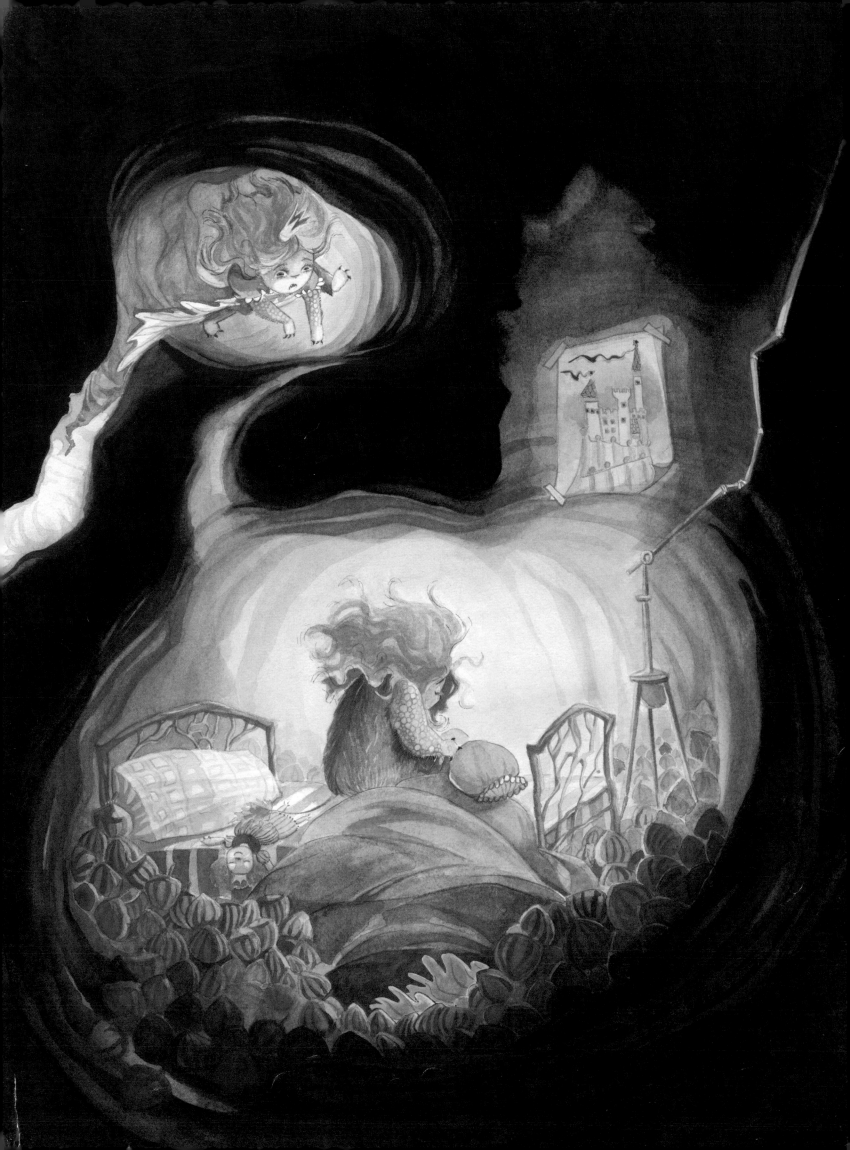

So the day after next

Up

Up

Up

one more time.

To the castle above

she made the long climb.

On the way up the path, a shadow arose.
Lala crept a bit closer and suddenly froze.

She saw the three princesses huddled in fear,
trapped by a wiffle, who grinned ear to ear.
With sour beast-breath the fiend growled out,

"MY!
I'M HUNGRY TODAY FOR
SWEET PRINCESS PIE!"

Lala turned, and she ran . . .

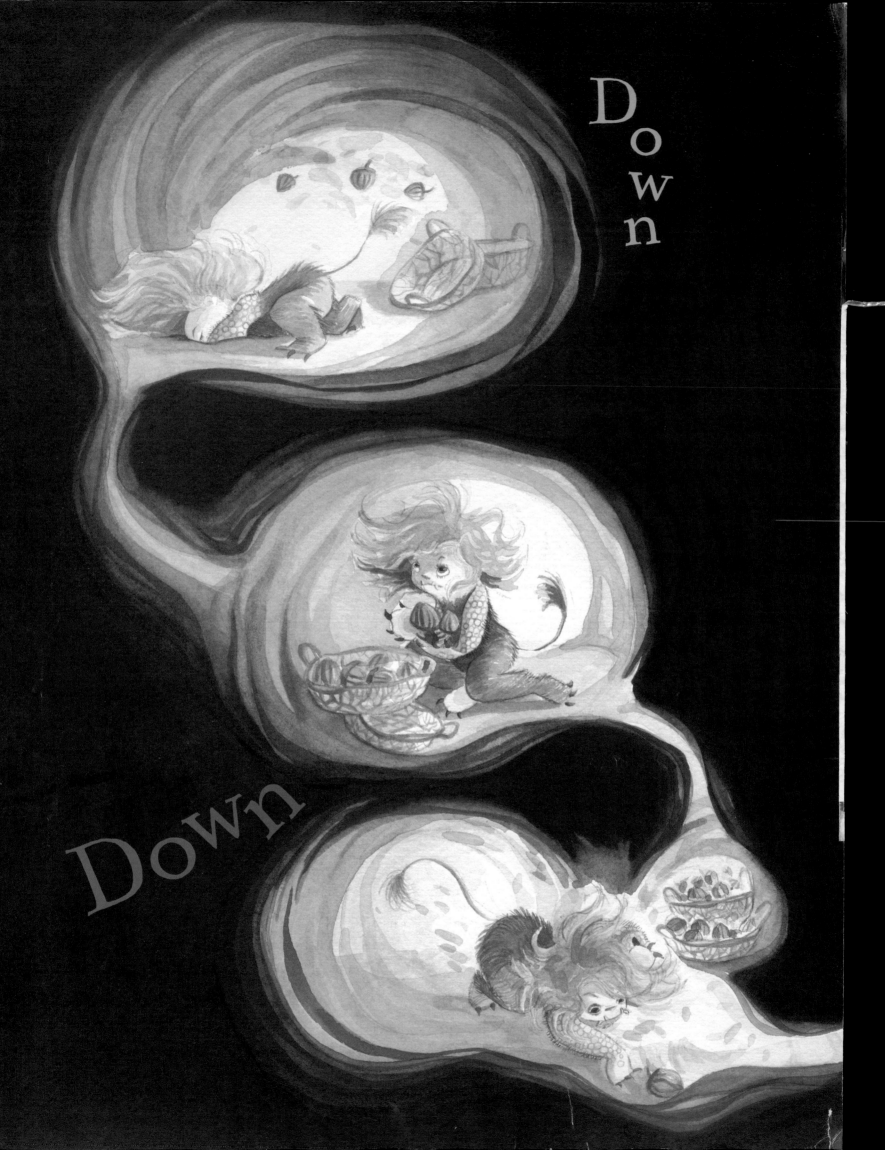

Down

far below.
Back to the caves where
krinkle nuts grow.

Said the wiffle, **"YOU FIRST, YOU LOOK TASTY TO ME.**
~~**AFTER THAT I'LL EAT YOU.**~~
~~**AND YOU'RE NUMBER THREE."**~~

"Hello, Mr. Wiffle!"

Lala called with no fear.

"If you're hungry, my krinkles are waiting right here!"

Now, wiffles love krinkles.

They eat them all day.

"DISHLISH!"

He crunched

as the girls ran away.

"Thank you, dear Lala,"
they cried with a fuss.
"We were wrong."
"We're so sorry."
"You're a princess, like us!"

Lala smiled and said,

"No, I'm proudly a gnome.

Thanks for the offer,

but it's time I went home."

Mom gave a big hug to her Star Who Shines Bright

and said, "Caves may be dark, but you bring in the light."

The once gloomy cavern now had a warm glow.

Feeling right with yourself will do that, you know.

There are all kinds of special; that's what she found true.

Lala's tale is now happy.

And yours should be too.